# POCKET TREASURY

DEAN

**MR. MEN    LITTLE MISS**

MR. MEN™ LITTLE MISS™ © THOIP (a Sanrio company)

**www.mrmen.com**

Mr. Men™ and Little Miss™
Copyright © 2012 THOIP (a Sanrio company). All rights reserved.
Printed and published under licence from
Price Stern Sloan, Inc., Los Angeles.
Original concept by Roger Hargreaves
Illustrated and written by Adam Hargreaves

This edition published in Great Britain in 2012 by Dean,
an imprint of Egmont UK Limited,
239 Kensington High Street, London W8 6SA

ISBN 978 0 6035 6673 8
49670/1
Printed in Singapore

# CONTENTS

# MR. GREEDY
## is helpfully heavy

Mr Greedy likes to eat.

And the more he eats the bigger he gets and the bigger he gets the heavier he becomes.

Which was a problem, as you will see.

Mr Greedy woke up and yawned and stretched.

CRACK!

BUMP!

The 'CRACK!' was the sound of Mr Greedy's bed breaking and the 'BUMP!' was the sound of Mr Greedy hitting the floor.

"Oh dear," said Mr Greedy.

Mr Greedy got up off the floor and went into the bathroom and ran a bath.

But when he got into the bath all the water got out.

There was not enough room in the bath for both Mr Greedy and the water!

"Oh dear," he said again.

Mr Greedy looked at himself in his mirror.

He had a wide mirror, but he was even wider and could not see very much of himself.

"Oh dear."

He went downstairs for breakfast.

As he waited for the bread to toast he let his hand rest on the loaf of bread.

And squashed it flat.

He even had heavy hands!

After a large breakfast of squashed toast he leant back in his chair.

There was another loud 'CRACK!' and 'BUMP!'
He found himself on the floor again.

"I wish I wasn't so heavy," he sighed to himself.

Now Mr Greedy had been invited to Mr Uppity's house for lunch.

So Mr Greedy squeezed through his front door and squeezed into his car.

He started the engine.

Then, with four loud bangs, all four tyres on his car burst.

BANG! BANG! BANG! BANG!

He had to get the bus.

But when he climbed on, the other end of the bus tipped up!

"I think you need to lose some weight," suggested the bus conductor.

As the bus drove off without him, Mr Greedy looked down at his large tummy.

"Oh dear," he sighed, not for the first time that day.

Mr Greedy had to walk all the way to
Mr Uppity's house.

He was very tired and very hot and very hungry
when he got there.

Mr Uppity lived in the biggest house in Bigtown.

Mr Uppity was very rich.

Mr Uppity answered the door.

"What do you want?" he demanded.

Mr Uppity was very rude.

"You invited me for lunch," said Mr Greedy.

"Oh yes," said Mr Uppity. "You'll have to wait.
I'm very busy."

"What are you doing?" asked Mr Greedy.

"Packing," answered Mr Uppity, and went up to
his bedroom.

Mr Greedy followed.

Mr Uppity's bedroom was full of suitcases and every suitcase was overflowing.

Mr Uppity went round the room trying to close them, but they were so full it was impossible.

"Don't just stand there, give me a hand," ordered Mr Uppity bossily.

Mr Greedy tried pushing a suitcase shut,
but it was no good.

Then he had an idea.

He sat on the lid of the suitcase and because
he was so heavy the suitcase closed.

"Brilliant," said Mr Uppity. "You can shut the rest."

Mr Greedy beamed.

For the first time in a very long time Mr Greedy had found something useful that he could do.

And on his way home Mr Greedy had an idea.

An idea that meant he could be useful every day.

He went to the local newspaper and placed an advertisement.

every after.  The End.

Going on Holiday?
Having trouble fitting
everything in your
suitcase?

**Then call**

**Mr. Greedy.**
The expert
suitcase squasher.

when he returned
said what a lovel

Disaster strikes a
the daisy above M
Small's house is
blown over in hig
winds.

Mr. Strong break
eating record by
eggs.  Ask how h
he said 'very stror

Little Miss Bossy
fell over laughing
which is very unu

Mr Greedy had found himself a job.

He went home, ate a huge supper to celebrate, went to bed and slept.

And do you know how he slept?

I'll tell you.

He slept ...

... heavily.

# MR. TICKLE
## in a tangle

Now, who does that extraordinarily long arm belong to?

Of course! Mr Tickle.

And Mr Tickle's long, long arms come in very handy.

They can reach kites caught in trees.

They can answer the phone when Mr Tickle is in the bath.

But, most importantly, they are splendidly perfect for tickling!

Tickling people around corners.

Tickling people through upstairs windows.

And even tickling people on the other side of letter boxes!

However, there are days when those extraordinarily long arms are not so handy.

Days when they are nothing but a nuisance.

Days like last Monday.

Mr Tickle was lying in bed eating breakfast when he heard his garden gate open.

It was Mr Stamp, the postman.

Quick as a flash Mr Tickle sent one of his long arms down the stairs to tickle Mr Stamp.

Or, that is what he intended to do, but somehow or other, his arm got tangled up in the banisters.

Poor Mr Tickle!

It took him an hour to untangle his arm!

The letter Mr Stamp had delivered was an invitation from Mr Uppity, for lunch at the Grand Hotel.

Mr Tickle took the bus to town and sat on the upper deck.

Mr Tickle sent one of his long arms down the stairs to tickle the bus driver, but, somehow or other, the ticket inspector trod on his arm!

OUCH!

Mr Tickle arrived at the Grand Hotel and rushed through the revolving door.

Or rather he tried to, but, somehow or other, his arms caught in the door.

The fire brigade had to be called out to untangle his arms, by which time he had missed lunch.

Poor Mr Tickle.

No lunch, and even worse, no tickles!

It was a very sad Mr Tickle who set off for home.

Suddenly he heard something.

He stopped. Somebody was approaching
from around the corner.

Mr Tickle smiled to himself.

And sent both his arms around the corner to
tickle that somebody.

But that somebody was Little Miss Naughty.

And she tied those extraordinarily long arms together in a knot!

When he got home, Mr Tickle fell back into his armchair.

What a terrible day.

Not one tickle!

Suddenly there was a knock at the door.

It was Little Miss Tiny.

Mr Tickle stretched out one of his extraordinarily long arms.

Well, one tickle was better than none.

Even if it was only a tiny tickle!

# MR. HAPPY
## finds a hobby

Mr Happy is a happy sort of fellow. He lives in Happyland which is a happy sort of place.

Behind his house there is a wood full of happy birds and on the other side of the wood there is a lake full of happy fish.

Now, one day, not that long ago, Mr Happy
went for a walk down through the wood.

As he came to the shore of the lake he heard
an unusual sound.

A sound that is seldom heard in Happyland.

It was the sound of somebody moaning
and grumbling.

Mr Happy peered round the trunk of a tree.

At the edge of the lake there was somebody fishing.

Fishing and grumbling.

And grumbling and fishing.

It was Mr Grumble.

"Good morning, Mr Grumble," said Mr Happy.

"Ssssh!" ssshed Mr Grumble.

"Sorry," whispered Mr Happy. "Have you caught anything?"

"Yes! I've caught a cold!" grumbled Mr Grumble.

"I've been sitting here all night. I hate fishing!"

"Then, why <u>are</u> you fishing?" asked Mr Happy.

"Because Mr Quiet said it was fun! And, you see I'm trying to find something I enjoy doing. Something I can do as a hobby."

"Hmmm," pondered Mr Happy. "I might be able to help. Come on, let's see if we can find you a hobby."

As they walked along, Mr Happy thought long and hard and as he thought Mr Grumble grumbled.

He grumbled about the noise the birds were making.

He grumbled about having to walk.

But most of all he grumbled about not having a hobby.

Grumble, grumble, grumble.

First of all they met Mr Rush in his car.
Mr Happy explained what they were doing.

"What's your hobby?" asked Mr Grumble.

"Speed!" said Mr Rush. "Hop in!"

And they did. Mr Grumble very quickly
decided that he did not like going fast.

Next they met Little Miss Giggles.

"What's your hobby?" asked Mr Grumble.

"I... tee hee... like... tee hee... giggling,"
giggled Little Miss Giggles.

So they went to the circus to see the clowns.

Little Miss Giggles giggled, Mr Happy laughed and
Mr Grumble... frowned!

"I hate custard pies," grumbled Mr Grumble.

It proved to be a very long day for Mr Happy.

They went everywhere.

To Little Miss Splendid's house.

But Mr Grumble did not like hats.

They went to Mr Mischief's house.

But Mr Grumble did not like practical jokes.

They bounced with Mr Bounce.

And they looked through keyholes with Mr Nosey.

But nothing was right. In fact, nothing was left.

Mr Happy had run out of ideas.

As the sun was setting, they saw Mr Impossible coming towards them down the lane.

"Now, if anybody can help us that somebody ought to be Mr Impossible," said Mr Happy.

"Hello," he said. "You're good at the impossible. Can you think of a hobby that Mr Grumble would enjoy?"

"That..." said Mr Impossible.

"Yes..." said Mr Happy and Mr Grumble together.

"...would be impossible," said Mr Impossible.

"Grrr!" growled Mr Grumble, and stomped off home.

It was whilst drinking a cup of tea the next morning that Mr Happy had an idea.

A perfectly obvious idea.

He rushed round to Mr Grumble's house.

"I've got it!" cried Mr Happy. "You can take up fishing."

"Fishing!? But I hate fishing."

"I know, but what do you do while you are fishing?" asked Mr Happy.

"I don't know."

"You grumble," said Mr Happy. "And what do you like doing most of all?"

"I like..." and then it dawned on Mr Grumble. "I like grumbling!"

Mr Grumble looked at Mr Happy and then for the first time in a very long time he smiled.

A very small smile, but a smile all the same.

# MR. NOSEY
## and the big surprise

Mr Nosey is the sort of person who does not mind his own business.

He minds everyone else's business!

He is as nosey as his nose is long.

If there is a keyhole to look through or a letter box to listen at you'll find Mr Nosey there looking or listening, and probably both.

One day while Mr Nosey was taking a walk through the wood on the other side of Tiddletown he heard a door shut.

"That's odd," he said to himself.

Mr Nosey peered around a tree and there was a wall. A wall that he had never noticed before.

Now, Mr Nosey can't go past a wall without knowing what is on the other side.

And rather handily this wall had a door in it. A small yellow door.

Mr Nosey being the nosey fellow he is could not resist taking a look.

He opened the door and peered around it.

On the other side of the wall was a tiny house with a yellow door.

Inside the house was a lift.

Mr Nosey got in the lift and pressed the button.

The lift went down.

And down.

And down.

And down, for what seemed like a very long time.

At the bottom the lift doors opened onto a long tunnel with a light at the end.

Mr Nosey set off down the tunnel.

By this time Mr Nosey was very curious.

He couldn't wait to see where the tunnel would lead.

At the end of the tunnel there was another small
yellow door.

And then another tunnel.

"There must be something really interesting
at the end," Mr Nosey said to himself,
as he hurried along.

He came to another door and then a long, winding staircase and another tunnel at the top.

Mr Nosey had quite lost track of time but he felt
sure that he was coming close to the end.

He finally came to yet another small, yellow door
just like all the others ... except this one
had a keyhole.

Mr Nosey peeked through the keyhole.

All he could see was a white room, so he opened the door and there was a white room.

Nothing else!

No furniture.

No carpets.

No pictures.

Just a white room.

Mr Nosey walked into the room.

He had never been so disappointed in all his life.

He turned to leave and it was then that he saw a note stuck to the back of the door.

And written on the note was:

TEE! HEE!

SIGNED: Mr Mischief

Mr Nosey groaned.

And went home ... the long way.

And now you know what to do if you ever
discover a small, yellow door.

Keep walking!

# MR. BUMP
## loses his memory

Mr Bump is the sort of person who is always having accidents.

Small accidents.

Medium sized accidents.

And big accidents.

Lots and lots of accidents.

One day Mr Bump got out of bed, or rather,
he fell out of bed as he did every morning.

He drew back the curtains and opened the window.

It was a beautiful day.

He leant on the window sill and breathed in deeply
and ... fell out of the window.

BUMP!

Mr Bump sat up and rubbed his head. And as
he rubbed, it dawned on him that he had
no idea where he was.

He had no idea whose garden he was sitting in.

He had no idea whose house he was sitting in
front of.

And he had no idea who he was.

Mr Bump had lost his memory.

Mr Bump walked up to his garden gate and looked down the lane.

Mr Muddle was passing by.

"Good afternoon," said Mr Muddle.

As you and I know, it was morning. But Mr Muddle, not surprisingly, always gets things in a muddle.

"I seem to have lost my memory," said Mr Bump. "Do you know what my name is?"

"You're Mr Careful," said Mr Muddle.

"Thank you," said Mr Bump.

Mr Bump went into town.

The first person he met was Mrs Packet the grocer, carrying an armful of groceries.

"Hello," said Mr Bump, "I'm Mr Careful, can I help?"

"Just the person! I need someone careful to deliver these eggs."

Mr Bump took the eggs from Mrs Packet and set off down the high street.

And because he was Mr Bump he slipped and fell on the eggs, breaking all of them.

"You're not all that careful, are you?" said Mrs Packet.

"Sorry," said Mr Bump.

He walked on past the dairy. Mr Bottle the manager came out.

"I'm looking for someone to drive the milk float," he said. "What's your name?"

"Mr Careful," replied Mr Bump.

"Perfect," said Mr Bottle. "I need someone careful to do the milk round."

Mr Bump set off down the road.

As he rounded the corner he hit the curb and the milk float turned over, smashing all the milk bottles.

"Well, that wasn't very carefully done, was it?" said Mr Bottle.

"Sorry," said Mr Bump.

Then he met Mr Brush the painter, who was up a ladder, painting.

"Hello," said Mr Bump. "I'm Mr Careful. Do you need a hand?"

"Yes please," replied Mr Brush. "I need someone careful to pass me that paint pot."

Mr Bump began to climb the ladder.

And being Mr Bump he fell off and the pot of paint landed on his head.

Mr Bump went for a walk.

"I don't understand it," he said to himself. "My name is Mr Careful, but I can't do anything carefully!"

It was then that he walked into a tree.

BUMP!

And bumped his head.

An apple fell out of the tree into his hand.

"That's odd, " he said to himself. "How did I get here? The last thing I remember is opening my bedroom window."

" ... And where did all this paint come from?"

You know, don't you?

Just at that moment Farmer Fields turned up.

"Careful ... " he called.

"That sounds familiar," said Mr Bump, and fell down the bank into the river.

# MR. TOPSY-TURVY
## the round way wrong

If Mr Topsy-Turvy can do something the wrong way round then you can be certain that he will.

Like the way he drives a car.

Which explains why you never see him driving a car.

... And why he travels by bus.

Mr Topsy-Turvy woke up early one morning.

He has a very topsy-turvy way of sleeping in bed as you can see.

He yawned and stretched and got up.

Then he went upstairs for breakfast.

That's right, Mr Topsy-Turvy's house is just as topsy-turvy as he is.

All his bedrooms are downstairs and his kitchen and living room are upstairs.

Mr Topsy-Turvy decided to have cornflakes for breakfast.

He opened the packet.

But being Mr Topsy-Turvy he didn't pour the cornflakes out, oh no, he poured the milk into the packet!

His meals tend to be very messy affairs.

After he had finished breakfast Mr Topsy-Turvy caught the bus into town. "One town for ticket, please," he said to the bus driver.

The bus driver scratched his head.

"Don't you mean, one ticket for town?" he said.

"Right that's," said Mr Topsy-Turvy.

Mr Topsy-Turvy speaks as topsy-turvily as everything else he does.

Now, this day was a rather special day for Mr Topsy-Turvy. He had been saving up to buy a new house.

He went into Mr Homes' Estate Agency and said, "I'd like new to house a buy."

Mr Homes knew Mr Topsy-Turvy quite well.

"You mean, you'd like to buy a new house?"

"Right that's," said Mr Topsy-Turvy, for the second time that day.

"If you wait outside the front I'll go and get my car," said Mr Homes.

And of course Mr Topsy-Turvy waited outside the back.

After Mr Homes eventually found him they set off in the car to look at some houses.

They looked at all sorts.

Tall, skinny houses.

Short, squat houses.

Even short, skinny houses, but Mr Topsy-Turvy didn't like any of them.

None of them seemed quite right to him.

As they were driving back to town Mr Topsy-Turvy suddenly shouted to Mr Homes to stop the car.

Well, what he actually said was, "Stop car the!" but Mr Homes knew what he meant.

On the other side of a hedge was the strangest house you have ever seen.

Everything was upside-down.

In fact, everything was topsy-turvy.

And I'm sure you can guess whose house it was.

"Now, house of that's the sort want I,"
said Mr Topsy-Turvy.

"But ... ," said Mr Homes, "But that's your house!"

"Right that's," said Mr Topsy-Turvy, for the third
time that day.

"But you can't move house into your own house!"
exclaimed Mr Homes. "That would be all the way
round wrong ... I mean the wrong way round."

Mr Topsy-Turvy grinned a huge grin.

"Exactly," he said.

# MR. SILLY
## gets the giggles

Mr Silly lives in a place called Nonsenseland where the grass is blue and the trees are red. Which you already know.

It is also a place where zebra crossings are spotty. Which you probably did not know.

In Nonsenseland you post letters in telephone boxes and you make phone calls from letter boxes.

And in Nonsenseland the umbrellas all have holes in them so that you know when it has stopped raining.

Which is utter nonsense, but not if your name is Mr Silly.

Now, one morning, last week, Mr Silly got up, put on his hat, brushed his teeth with soap, as usual, polished his shoes with toothpaste, as usual, and went down to breakfast.

For breakfast Mr Silly had fried eggs and custard, as usual, and a cup of hot, milky marmalade, as usual.

After breakfast he went out into his garden. The day before Mr Silly had bought a tree, but as he looked at the tree he realised that he did not have a hole to plant it in.

So he went to the hardware shop.

"Good morning," said Mr Silly. "I would like to buy a hole."

"Sorry," said the sales assistant, "we're all out of holes. Sold the last one yesterday."

"Bother," said Mr Silly.

He decided there was nothing for it but to go in search of a hole.

He walked and he walked and he walked.

Eventually Mr Silly stopped walking and looked down at his feet.

"That's odd," he said, "this grass is green."

"Of course it is," said a voice behind him. "Grass is always green."

"Who are you?" asked Mr Silly.

"Little Miss Wise."

"I'm Mr Silly. Could you tell me where I am?"

"You're in Sensibleland," said Miss Wise.

Mr Silly had walked so far that he had walked right out of Nonsenseland.

"I'm looking for a hardware shop," said Mr Silly. "Can you help?"

"Certainly," said Miss Wise. "Follow me."

As they walked along Mr Silly looked about him.

He had never seen anywhere like it. The grass was green, the trees were green, even the hedges were green.

They came to a zebra crossing. A stripey zebra crossing.

Mr Silly chuckled, and then he giggled and then he laughed out loud.

"Why are you laughing?" asked Miss Wise.

"The... hee hee... zebra crossing... ha ha... is stripey," laughed Mr Silly.

"What else would a zebra crossing be?" said Miss Wise.

"Spotty! Of course!" said Mr Silly, wiping the tears from his eyes.

"How silly," said Miss Wise.

They set off again and the further they went the more Mr Silly laughed.

He laughed when he saw someone posting a letter in a letterbox.

He laughed when he saw someone using a phone in a telephone box.

And he laughed when he saw an umbrella without holes in it.

Eventually they came to Miss Bolt's Hardware Shop.

"Good afternoon," said Mr Silly. "I would like to buy a hole."

"A hole?" questioned Miss Bolt.

"Yes, big enough to plant a tree in," explained Mr Silly.

Miss Bolt sniggered.

Miss Wise chortled.

And then they burst out laughing.

"I've never heard anything so absurd," laughed Miss Bolt. "But I do have something that may help, though."

That evening Mr Silly invited his friend Mr Nonsense for supper and told him all about his day in Sensibleland.

Mr Nonsense laughed so hard he fell off his chair!

"...and then," continued Mr Silly, "Miss Bolt gave me a spade. A spade! Why in the world would I want to buy a spade when all I wanted was a hole!"

"Heehee... that's... ha ha... ridiculous!" laughed Mr Nonsense. "What's for pudding?"

"Spam roly poly," answered Mr Silly.

"Oh goody," said Mr Nonsense. "My favourite."

# MR. FUNNY
## upsets Mr. Fussy

Mr Funny lives in a teapot shaped house.

He drives a shoe shaped car.

And he has a teacup shaped bath.

Mr Fussy lives in a very ordinary house and drives a very ordinary car and his bath is a very ordinary bath.

Mr Funny is a very funny fellow.

So funny that when he pulls one of his funny faces you can't help but laugh.

Mr Fussy is very serious.

Very serious about keeping everything neat and tidy and spic and span.

Now Mr Funny lives at the very end of Long Lane and Mr Fussy lives half way down Long Lane.

So whenever Mr Funny goes out for a drive in his shoe car he has to pass by Mr Fussy's house.

Every time that Mr Funny passes Mr Fussy he pulls one of his funny faces.

And as hard as he tries, Mr Fussy can't help laughing.

He laughs so much that he ends up having accidents.

Like the time he was mowing his lawn.

He laughed so much he ruined all his
nice straight lines.

And when he was cleaning his windows.

He laughed so much he fell off his ladder
and squashed his prize pumpkin.

And he burnt his shoe laces while he
was ironing them.

Mr Fussy was fed up.

But then he had an idea.

He put up a sign on the lane just before his house.

It read: 'Please Beep Your Horn'.

"That should work," he said to himself.

The idea was that if Mr Funny beeped his horn
Mr Fussy would have some warning and he
could stop whatever it was he was doing.

The next day Mr Funny was driving down the lane as usual when he saw Mr Fussy's sign.

So he beeped his car's horn and stopped his shoe car outside Mr Fussy's gate.

Mr Fussy had not reckoned on the sound that Mr Funny's car horn would make.

It doesn't go BEEP.

Oh no, it sounds like somebody making a very loud raspberry noise.

'THURRRPT!!' went the car horn.

Mr Fussy was outside in his coal bunker.
Stacking his coal in neat rows.

Mr Fussy didn't like untidy piles of coal!

When Mr Fussy heard the sound Mr Funny's car made he started to giggle.

And then he chuckled.

And then he laughed.

And he laughed so much he fell over into his neatly stacked coal.

Once he had recovered from his laughing fit
he stormed out of the coal bunker.

He was covered from head to foot in coal.

And he was furious.

He stormed over to Mr Funny.

"That's the most ridiculous car horn I've ever heard," he yelled at Mr Funny.

"There's a reason for that," Mr Funny explained. "It's because it's not a car horn, it's a ..."

" ... shoe-horn, ha ha ha, hee hee hee," he laughed.

And even Mr Fussy had to admit that was quite funny.

Wouldn't you agree?

**THE END**

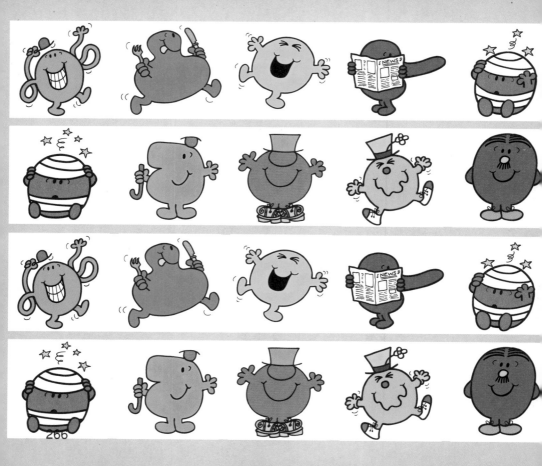